NEVILLE

Based on *The Railway Series* by the Rev. W. Awdry

D0608590

Illustrations by
Robin Davies and Jerry Smith

EGMONT

EGMONT

We bring stories to life

First published in Great Britain in 2007
by Egmont UK Limited
239 Kensington High Street, London W8 6SA
All Rights Reserved

Thomas the Tank Engine & Friends™

A BRITT ALLCROFT COMPANY PRODUCTION

Based on The Railway Series by The Reverend W Awdry
© 2007 Gullane (Thomas) LLC. A HIT Entertainment Company

Thomas the Tank Engine & Friends and Thomas & Friends are trademarks of Gullane (Thomas) Limited.
Thomas the Tank Engine & Friends and Design is Reg. US. Pat. & Tm. Off.

ISBN 978 1 4052 2939 5
1 3 5 7 9 10 8 6 4 2
Printed in Great Britain

The Forest Stewardship Council (FSC) is an international, non-governmental organisation
dedicated to promoting responsible management of the world's forests. FSC operates a
system of forest certification and product labelling that allows consumers to identify
wood and wood-based products from well managed forests.

For more information about Egmont's paper buying policy please visit www.egmont.co.uk/ethicalpublishing

For more information about the FSC please visit their website at www.fsc.uk.org

This is a story about Neville, a little engine who just wanted to be friends. But Thomas and the others wouldn't give him a chance, and that got them all into trouble…

One morning, The Fat Controller made an announcement.

"A new engine has arrived on the Island!" he said.

"His name is Neville. You must all make him feel welcome."

"I wonder what this Neville will be like?" Thomas said to Emily.

"I hope he's a steamie like us!" Emily replied.

Later that day, Thomas had stopped at a signal when the Signalman called down to him.

"The bridge ahead is unsafe!" he said. "It needs mending before any engines can cross it.

"You must go to the Docks and collect some iron to repair the bridge."

At the Docks, 'Arry and Bert were with Neville, the new engine. Neville was a steamie, but he had a square body like a diesel.

'Arry and Bert were feeling naughty.

"We'll help you shunt those trucks," they said.

But they pushed Neville hard into the trucks!

The diesels laughed. Neville looked sad.

"It's not our fault if you're a silly Steamie!" oiled Bert. And they laughed even harder.

When Thomas arrived at the Docks, he thought he saw 'Arry and Bert laughing with Neville.

"There's the new engine," Thomas thought. "He seems to be friends with the Diesels. How strange!"

Thomas chuffed off to Knapford station.

"We'd better be careful of that new engine," he warned James at the platform. "I saw him laughing with 'Arry and Bert at the Docks!"

James was shocked. A steamie friends with diesels?

He chugged off to take on water. "That new engine Neville is best friends with the diesels," he puffed when Percy passed by. "He doesn't like steamies. Thomas told me!"

Later, Percy met Emily at a red signal.

"Don't go near Neville the new engine," he told her. "The diesels have told him to biff into steamies. James heard it from Thomas!"

When Thomas arrived at Crovansgate, The Fat Controller was there.

"I have a very important job for you," he boomed. "You must warn all the engines not to cross the bridge until it is repaired."

Thomas felt proud. It was a Really Useful job.

Then he heard a whistle. Someone was coming!

He had to warn them.

But when Thomas saw it was Neville, he forgot all about his important job.

"He's pulling Annie and Clarabel!" Thomas sulked crossly. "They're my coaches, not his!"

"Hello!" puffed Neville, perkily.

"I'm not talking to you!" Thomas huffed.

Neville was puzzled and sad.

When Emily pulled in next to him, Neville gave her a big, friendly smile. He hoped she would be nicer than Thomas!

Emily wheeshed out steam. "It's no use trying to make friends with me," she said, grandly. "I know you're going to biff into all the steamies, just like the diesels told you to!"

Neville didn't know why she was being so horrid to him. But the Stationmaster blew his whistle, and Neville had to chug sadly away.

Then Emily saw Thomas.

"Thanks for warning us about Neville," she said. "Percy told me what you told James."

Thomas was very surprised.

"I only said I saw Neville with the diesels!" he cried.

But before Emily could answer, Toby arrived. "Have you heard?" he puffed. "Salty saw 'Arry and Bert be horrible to Neville at the Docks!"

So the diesels weren't Neville's friends at all!

All of a sudden, Thomas remembered where Neville was going.

"Neville's heading for the broken bridge!" he cried. "I must stop him!"

Neville was speeding along. Suddenly he saw a barrier on the track. He slammed on his brakes, but it was too late. His front wheels went over the broken end of the bridge!

Thomas came racing up and saw what had happened. He knew it was all his fault!

Then he had an idea. He would pull Neville back!

Thomas steamed slowly and carefully on to the bridge. He gently bumped Clarabel, and Thomas' Driver coupled Clarabel to him.

Thomas was very scared. Slowly and steadily, he began to pull Neville back from the edge.

The bridge creaked. Thomas had to hurry.

With one big puff, he pulled Neville to safety!

"Thanks," whistled Neville. "What a relief!"

"I should have warned you," puffed Thomas. "But I was too busy believing silly stories. I thought you didn't like steamies. Can you forgive me?"

"Oh yes!" peeped Neville. "Let's be friends!"

Thomas gave Neville a long happy "Peep! Peep!". From now on, he wanted to be the best friend Neville had ever had!

The Thomas Story Library is THE definitive collection of stories about Thomas and ALL his Friends.

5 more Thomas Story Library titles will be chuffing into your local bookshop in August 2007:

Rocky
Rosie
Dennis
Alfie
The Fat Controller

And there are even more
Thomas Story Library books to follow later!
So go on, start your Thomas Story Library NOW!

A Fantastic Offer for Thomas the Tank Engine Fans!

1 THOMAS TOKEN

Thomas

In every Thomas Story Library book like this one, you will find a special token. Collect 6 Thomas tokens and we will send you a brilliant Thomas poster, and a double-sided bedroom door hanger! Simply tape a £1 coin in the space above, and fill out the form overleaf.

TO BE COMPLETED BY AN ADULT

To apply for this great offer, ask an adult to complete the coupon below and send it with a pound coin and 6 tokens, to:
THOMAS OFFERS, PO BOX 715, HORSHAM RH12 5WG

☐ Please send a Thomas poster and door hanger. I enclose 6 tokens plus a £1 coin. (Price includes P&P)

Fan's name..

Address..

....Postcode...................................

Date of birth..

Name of parent/guardian...

Signature of parent/guardian...

Please allow 28 days for delivery. Offer is only available while stocks last. We reserve the right to change the terms of this offer at any time and we offer a 14 day money back guarantee. This does not affect your statutory rights.

☐ Data Protection Act: If you do not wish to receive other similar offers from us or companies we recommend, please tick this box. Offers apply to UK only.